何 不 浅 尝 辄 止

joy of first glimpse

浅尝诗丛

被点燃的春天

传世风物诗

·中英双语·

［美］罗伯特·弗罗斯特 等 著

凤凰诗歌出版中心 编　李小蕾 译

图书在版编目（CIP）数据

被点燃的春天 : 传世风物诗 / (美) 罗伯特 · 弗罗斯特等著 ; 李小蕾译 . -- 南京 : 江苏凤凰文艺出版社，2023.9

(浅尝诗丛)

ISBN 978-7-5594-7910-5

Ⅰ . ①被… Ⅱ . ①罗… ②李… Ⅲ . ①诗集 - 美国 - 现代 Ⅳ . ① I712.25

中国国家版本馆 CIP 数据核字 (2023) 第 157398 号

被点燃的春天：传世风物诗

(美) 罗伯特 · 弗罗斯特等　著　李小蕾　译

出 版 人　张在健
责任编辑　王娱瑶　徐　辰
装帧设计　徐芳芳
责任印制　刘　巍
出版发行　江苏凤凰文艺出版社
　　　　　南京市中央路 165 号，邮编：210009
出版社网址　http://www.jswenyi.com
印　　刷　江苏凤凰新华印务集团有限公司
开　　本　880 毫米 ×1230 毫米　1/32
印　　张　6.75
字　　数　110 千字
版　　次　2023 年 9 月第 1 版　2023 年 9 月第 1 次印刷
标准书号　ISBN 978-7-5594-7910-5
定　　价　42.00 元

CONTENT

目录

Star
星星

Rain
雨

Wind
风

Moon
月亮

Water
流水

Season
四季

Plant

草木

Animal
动物

City
城市

Sea

大海

Star

星星

Stars

by Sara Teasdale

Alone in the night
On a dark hill,
With pines around me
Spicy and still,

And a heaven full of stars
Over my head,
White and topaz
And misty red;

Myriads with beating
Hearts of fire
That aeons
Cannot vex or tire;

Up the dome of heaven
Like a great hill,
I watch them marching

Stately and still,

And I know that I

Am honored to be

Witness

Of so much majesty.

星星

[美国]萨拉·提斯黛尔

孤零零的夜晚
黑漆漆的山顶，
四周遍布松树
芳香又寂静；

天空缀满星星
就在我的头顶，
有洁白和莹黄
还有雾红；

无尽的星光闪烁
像心脏火热跳动，
漫长的时光悠悠
不曾疲倦或哀愁；

向着天穹进发
仿佛攀登峻岭，
注视它们前进

庄重又安静；

我深深明白，

得以见证

如此壮观的景象，

是我三生有幸。

To the Evening Star

by William Blake

Thou fair hair'd angel of the evening,

Now, while the sun rests on the mountains light,

Thy bright torch of love; Thy radiant crown

Put on, and smile upon our evening bed!

Smile on our loves; and when thou drawest the

Blue curtains, scatter thy silver dew

On every flower that shuts its sweet eyes

In timely sleep. Let thy west wind sleep on

The lake; speak silence with thy glimmering eyes

And wash the dusk with silver. Soon, full, soon,

Dost thou withdraw; Then, the wolf rages wide,

And the lion glares thro' the dun forest.

The fleece of our flocks are covered with

Thy sacred dew; Protect them with thine influence.

007

致昏星

[英国] 威廉 · 布莱克

你是夜晚的金发天使，
此刻，日薄西山，点亮
你明亮的爱之火把，把你灿烂的皇冠
戴上，把微笑投向我们夜晚安睡的床！
对着我们的爱微笑吧；当你拉上
蓝色的窗帘，把银色的露水洒在
每一朵紧闭着甜蜜双眼的花上，
让她们按时入睡。让你的西风在
湖面上酣睡，用你闪烁的眼睛沉默地诉说，
用你的银辉冲刷黄昏。快了，圆满了，就快了，
你就要把窗帘完全闭合。彼时，狼群已跃跃欲试，
狮子也透过茂密的森林观望。
以你神圣的甘露庇护我们的羊群吧；
把它们置于你的羽翼之下。

Evening Star

by Edgar Allan Poe

'Twas noontide of summer,
And mid-time of night;
And stars in their orbits,
Shone pale, thro' the light
Of the brighter, cold moon,
'Mid planets her slaves,
Herself in the Heavens,
Her beam on the waves.
I gazed awhile
On her cold smile;
Too cold—too cold for me—
There pass'd, as a shroud,
A fleecy cloud,
And I turn'd away to thee,
Proud Evening Star,
In thy glory afar,
And dearer thy beam shall be;
For joy to my heart

Is the proud part

Thou bearest in Heaven at night,

And more I admire

Thy distant fire,

Than that colder, lowly light.

昏星

[美国] 埃德加 · 爱伦 · 坡

正值夏日过半，

夜晚也走过中点；

群星在各自的轨道，

苍白地闪耀，映衬着

明亮清冽的月亮，

它们都是她的奴仆，

月亮高悬于天空，

光芒映照着海浪。

我对着她清冷的笑容

凝视了良久；

太冷了——于我而言太冷了——

一片浮云飘过，

像一袭长袍，

然后我转身望向你，

骄傲的昏星，

你遥远的璀璨，

比月光更亲切；

你为我的心带来欢畅

这胜过了一切。

你在夜空灼烧，

比起那轮无足轻重的冷月，

你在远方燃起的火焰

更让我心驰神往。

Bright Star, Would I Were Steadfast as Thou Art

by John Keats

Bright star, would I were steadfast as thou art—
Not in lone splendour hung aloft the night
And watching, with eternal lids apart,
Like nature's patient, sleepless Eremite,
The moving waters at their priest like task
Of pure ablution round earth's human shores,
Or gazing on the new soft-fallen mask
Of snow upon the mountains and the moors—
No—yet still steadfast, still unchangeable,
Pillow'd upon my fair love's ripening breast,
To feel for ever its soft fall and swell,
Awake for ever in a sweet unrest,
Still, still to hear her tender-taken breath,
And so live ever—or else swoon to death.

明亮的星，多么希望自己像你一样坚定

[英国] 约翰 · 济慈

明亮的星，多么希望自己像你一样坚定，
但我不愿独自高悬于夜空
凝望着，永远无法闭上眼睛，
如同自然界耐心又不眠的修士，
翻涌的海浪，执行着牧师的任务
用圣水冲刷人间的海岸，
或注视着新落的、绵软的雪，
高山和洼地上层层叠叠的雪——
不——我只愿像你一样坚定，亘古不变，
以爱人丰润的胸脯作枕头，
永远感受它柔软的起伏，
醒来时心中永远甜蜜如小鹿乱撞，
一直，一直听着她温润的呼吸，
就这样活着，或在昏睡中离去。

Lost Star

by Rabindranath Tagore

When the creation was new and all the stars shone in their first splendor, the gods held their assembly in the sky and sang "Oh, the picture of perfection! the joy unalloyed!"

But one cried of a sudden
—"It seems that somewhere there is a break in the chain of light and one of the stars has been lost."

The golden string of their harp snapped,
their song stopped, and they cried in dismay
—"Yes, that lost star was the best,
she was the glory of all heavens!"

From that day the search is unceasing for her,
and the cry goes on from one to the other
that in her the world has lost its one joy!

Only in the deepest silence of night the stars smile and whisper among themselves
—"Vain is this seeking! unbroken perfection is over all!"

丢失的星星

[印度] 罗宾德拉纳特 · 泰戈尔

当天地伊始，群星初次绽放光芒
诸神在天上济济一堂，齐声歌唱
“哦，完美的画面！纯真的欢畅！”

但是，其中一位突然大叫
——“光链里好像断了一处，
一颗星星不见了踪影。”

他们竖琴的金弦骤然断裂，
他们停止了歌唱，沮丧地喊叫
——“是的，丢失的那颗星星最为动人，
她是天国全部的荣耀！”

从那天起就开始了无休无止的寻找，
口口相传，声声哀叹
这世界因她的消失而失去了某种欢笑！

只有夜深人静之时

群星才低声私语、窃窃说笑

——“这样的寻找真是徒劳！世界早已完美，什么也不缺少！”

Summer Stars

by Carl Sandburg

Bend low again, night of summer stars.

So near you are, sky of summer stars,

So near, a long arm man can pick off stars,

Pick off what he wants in the sky bowl,

So near you are, summer stars,

So near, strumming, strumming,

So lazy and hum-strumming.

夏日繁星

[美国] 卡尔 · 桑德堡

又俯下身来，缀满夏日繁星的夜晚。

你近在咫尺，布满夏日繁星的天空，

如此迫近，长臂之人可摘得星辰，

在星空的碗碟里捡拾他的心头所好，

近在咫尺，夏日繁星，

如此之近，弹奏呀，弹奏，

懒洋洋地，轻声弹奏。

Stars Wheel in Purple

by Hilda Doolittle

Stars wheel in purple, yours is not so rare
as Hesperus, nor yet so great a star
as bright Aldeboran or Sirius,
nor yet the stained and brilliant one of War;

stars turn in purple, glorious to the sight;
yours is not gracious as the Pleiads are
nor as Orion's sapphires, luminous;

yet disenchanted, cold, imperious face,
when all the others blighted, reel and fall,
your star, steel-set, keeps lone and frigid tryst
to freighted ships, baffled in wind and blast.

群星在紫光里旋转

[美国] 希尔达 · 杜利特尔

群星在紫光里旋转，你的星辰
不像长庚那样罕见，也不似
闪亮的金牛或天狼那样耀眼，
又不如血染的战神那般辉煌；

群星在紫光里流转，景色壮观；
你的星辰不像昴宿那样优雅，
也不似猎户蓝宝石般的光芒璀璨；

然而当其他所有的星辰颓萎、衰败，
你那张清醒、冷漠、高傲的脸，
岿然不动，为风暴中被困的货船
安排单独的会面。

Rain
雨

Spring Rain

by Sara Teasdale

I thought I had forgotten,
But it all came back again
To-night with the first spring thunder
In a rush of rain.

I remembered a darkened doorway
Where we stood while the storm swept by,
Thunder gripping the earth
And lightning scrawled on the sky.

The passing motor busses swayed,
For the street was a river of rain,
Lashed into little golden waves
In the lamp light's stain.

With the wild spring rain and thunder
My heart was wild and gay;
Your eyes said more to me that night

Than your lips would ever say…

I thought I had forgotten,

But it all came back again

To-night with the first spring thunder

In a rush of rain.

春雨

[美国] 萨拉·提斯黛尔

我以为已经全然忘却，
但是回忆如潮水般涌来。
今晚它伴着第一声春雷，
和瓢泼大雨一同到来。

我犹记得在那黑暗的门廊，
你我并肩站立，外面雨打风吹，
雷声震撼着大地，
而闪电从天空蜿蜒划过。

路过的汽车左摇右摆，
因为街道已变成雨水汇流的河，
在路灯的晕染下，
溅起小小的金色浪花。

伴着狂野的春雨和春雷，
我的心里溢满狂喜；
你的眼睛在那晚诉说了很多，

比你的嘴唇吐露的还多……

我以为已经全然忘却，

谁知回忆如潮水般涌来。

今晚它伴着第一声春雷，

和瓢泼大雨一同到来。

The Fitful Alternations of The Rain

by Percy Bysshe Shelley

The fitful alternations of the rain,

When the chill wind, languid as with pain

Of its own heavy moisture, here and there,

Drives through the gray and beamless atmosphere.

时断时续的雨

[英国] 珀西 · 比希 · 雪莱

时断时续的雨,
寒风无精打采地吹过,仿佛一身伤痕。
沉郁的湿气，遍布四处，
穿越黯淡无光的大气层。

Bells in the Rain

by Elinor Wylie

Sleep falls, with limpid drops of rain,
Upon the steep cliffs of the town.
Sleep falls; men are at peace again
While the small drops fall softly down.

The bright drops ring like bells of glass,
Thinned by the wind, and lightly blown;
Sleep cannot fall on peaceful grass
So softly as it falls on stone.

Peace falls unheeded on the dead
Asleep; they have had deep peace to drink;
Upon a live man's bloody head,
It falls most tenderly, I think.

雨中的铃铛

[美国] 埃莉诺 · 怀利

睡意沉沉，伴着清澈的雨滴，
落在城镇的悬崖峭壁。
睡意沉沉，人们重归平静，
小小的雨滴温柔地洒落遍地。

透亮的雨滴如玻璃铃铛叮咚作响
在阵阵风中，被丝丝吹散；
睡意无法像落在石头上那样，
轻柔地拥抱平静的草地。

平静默然地落在长眠的死者身上，
他们已经拥有彻底的平静去痛饮；
当平静落在一个生者血淋淋的头上，
我觉得才是它最为温柔的时刻。

Soft Rain

by Karle Wilson Baker

There is room for ladies in a world that holds soft rain,
For delicate, undefended beauty
And gentleness.
There is room for slender young things, virgin-wistful,
With minds like bridal veils;
There is room for brittle old-lady minds
That function like the tinkling of tea-cups.
We have been too long blurry with rain,
They say,
And they are doubtless right:
It is the hour for biting wind and stabbing sunshine.
But I have walked in the soft rain today;
I have seen the mist
Sifting through the black mantilla of the bare elm;
There was in it eternal beauty —
It wrapped my heart in peace.

And it was shown unto me
That there will always be room for ladies — a little
room —
In a world that wearies, sometimes,
Of its hausfrau harvest-zeal for corn and squashes,
Of the feminist fury of its Wind-Valkyries;
That lapses, even,
From its male salt and sleet and thunder
Into moods of rain,
Soft rain.

细雨蒙蒙

[美国]卡尔·威尔逊·贝克

细雨蒙蒙的世界里有属于淑女的地方，
有属于一切精致的、不设防的美
与温柔的地方。
细雨蒙蒙的世界里有属于纤细女孩的地方，带着思春的感伤，
满怀愁绪仿佛新娘的面纱；
细雨蒙蒙的世界里还有属于迟暮女人的地方，
她们易碎的头脑发出茶杯碰撞的叮当声。
我们早已被细雨弄得糊里糊涂，
她们说。
她们无疑是对的：
是时候迎接刺骨的寒风和刺目的阳光了。
然而当我今天在细雨蒙蒙里走过，
我看见了薄雾
抚过光秃秃的榆树上黑色的螳螂；
它的身上凝结了永恒的美——
把我的心包裹在平静中。
这一切向我揭示了

永远有一块地方是属于淑女的，哪怕只是一块小小的地方。

这个世界，会在某些时刻，
厌倦了期盼玉米和南瓜的丰收，
厌倦了武神般狂怒的女权主义；
它甚至背离了
阳刚的汗水、雨雪和雷电
融入细雨的心境里，
融入细雨蒙蒙里。

The Laughter of the Rain

by James Whitcomb Riley

The rain sounds like a laugh to me—
A low laugh poured out limpidly.

MY very soul smiles as I listen to
The low, mysterious laughter of the rain,
Poured musically over heart and brain
Till sodden care, soaked with it through and through,
Sinks; and, with wings wet with it as with dew,
My spirit flutters up, with every stain
Rinsed from its plumage, and as white again
As when the old laugh of the rain was new.
Then laugh on, happy Rain! laugh louder yet!—
Laugh out in torrent-bursts of watery mirth;
Unlock thy lips of purple cloud, and let
Thy liquid merriment baptize the earth,
And wash the sad face of the world, and set
The universe to music dripping-wet!

雨水的笑声

[美国] 詹姆斯 · 惠特科姆 · 莱利

对我来说，雨声就像笑声——
低沉的笑声清澈地涌出。

我的灵魂在微笑，当我倾听
雨水那低沉又神秘的笑声，
它宛如音符倾泻而出，流进心田和头脑
直到湿透，一遍遍地浸润全身，
沉落；翅膀湿漉漉的，像挂着露珠，
我的灵魂振动双翅，羽毛上的每个污点
都被雨水冲刷干净，洁白一新，
仿佛雨水古老的笑声焕发了新的生命。
继续畅快地笑吧，快乐的雨！再笑得肆意一些——
在奔涌的快乐里放声大笑；
张开你紫色云朵的嘴唇，
用你流动的欢乐给大地受洗，
洗净世界那张悲伤的面庞，为
宇宙开启乐章，湿漉漉的乐章！

In Time of Silver Rain

by Langston Hughes

In time of silver rain
The earth puts forth new life again,
Green grasses grow
And flowers lift their heads,
And over all the plain
The wonder spreads.

Of Life,
Of Life,
Of Life!

In time of silver rain
The butterflies lift silken wings
To catch a rainbow cry,
And trees put forth new leaves to sing
In joy beneath the sky.
As down the roadway
Passing boys and girls

Go singing, too,

In time of silver rain

When spring

And life,

Are new.

银色细雨降临的时候

[美国]兰斯顿·休斯

银色细雨降临的时候，
大地又焕发生机，
青草生长，
花儿也仰起它们的头，
遍布整个平原，
奇迹正在上演。

生命的奇迹，
生命的奇迹，
生命的奇迹！

银色细雨降临的时候，
蝴蝶抬起丝滑的翅膀，
去捕捉彩虹的鸣叫，
树木抽出新叶去歌唱，
在天穹下欢乐地歌唱。
这时路边，
走过男孩们和女孩们，

他们也在边走边唱，

在银色细雨降临的时候，

当春光和生命，

焕然一新的时候。

June Rain

by Louise Driscoll

After the rain syringa bends
With scented blossoms at the ends
Of all its curving boughs. I think
That Pan himself might pause to drink
At such a fountain as I see.
The heavy headed peony
Drops silken petals, rosy sweet,
Upon a carpet for my feet.
And still the long wisteria drips
Its languid blossoms where the bee
In drowsiest contentment sips
From the deep wells of sweet that he
Has come so far to find. The rain
Sent him to hiding; with the sun
He shakes his pollen laden thighs
And lifts his strong, frail wings and flies
To see what harm the rain has done,
And tries the blossoms, one by one.

The meadow grass is growing long
It's silvered with the drops that cling
Like note that follows note in song
Or crystal beads upon a string.

There's beauty of the moon and sun,
And close of day and day begun,
And I have sung the Milky Way
And shining river, cool and gray,
And hills that are so near to me
I count them in my family;
But of the joys that I have had
In gifts the years bring back again,
Year after year to make me glad,
I love the clean green after rain
When yet there is no rust or stain
On any leaf, but all things are
As if we lived on some new star.

六月的雨

[美国]露易丝·德里斯科尔

雨后，丁香微微颔首，
所有弯曲的枝头
都开出芬芳的花朵。我觉得
连牧神都会停步啜饮
我看到的这一座喷泉。
沉甸甸的芍药
抖落柔软的花瓣，甜蜜的粉色
掉在我的脚垫上。
还有长长的紫藤垂下
散漫的花苞，供蜜蜂
在慵懒的满足中吮吸。
他飞了很久，才飞到
这些甜蜜的深井。雨水
让他不得不躲避；雨过天晴，
他摇晃着沾满花粉的大腿，
抬起他有力又脆弱的翅膀，飞过去
看看雨水造成了什么影响，
然后一朵接一朵，继续品尝着花香。

草地上的草儿在疯长。
它被银色的水滴包裹着，
就像一首歌中音符连着音符，
或者一根绳子上串起的水晶珠。

月亮和太阳自有大美，
黄昏和黎明也各有大美，
我歌唱过银河与闪亮的河水
冰凉的灰色河水，
还有近旁的小山，
我把它们也算作家庭成员；
然而在所有历经的欢乐中，
在岁月一次次带回的礼物中，
年复一年使我欢欣的，
还是雨后这苍翠的绿色。
所有的叶片都褪去了，
锈斑和污渍，一切崭新得仿佛
我们生活在某个新的星球上。

Wind
风

Wind

by Amy Lowell

He shouts in the sails of the ships at sea,

He steals the down from the honeybee,

He makes the forest trees rustle and sing,

He twirls my kite till it breaks its string.

Laughing, dancing, sunny wind,

Whistling, howling, rainy wind,

North, South, East and West,

Each is the wind I like the best.

He calls up the fog and hides the hills,

He whirls the wings of the great windmills,

The weathercocks love him and turn to discover

His whereabouts -- but he's gone, the rover!

Laughing, dancing, sunny wind,

Whistling, howling, rainy wind,

North, South, East and West,

Each is the wind I like the best.

The pine trees toss him their cones with glee,

The flowers bend low in courtesy,

Each wave flings up a shower of pearls,

The flag in front of the school unfurls.

Laughing, dancing, sunny wind,

Whistling, howling, rainy wind,

North, South, East and West,

Each is the wind I like the best.

风

[美国] 艾米·洛威尔

他在海上的船帆里吼叫，

他从蜜蜂那里偷来绒毛，

他让森林的树木沙沙作响地欢歌，

他吹动我的风筝直到它断了线索。

笑啊，跳啊，晴天的风，

呼啸啊，咆哮啊，雨天的风，

无论东风西风还是南风北风，

每一种风都是我最爱的风。

他呼唤迷雾，隐藏山丘，

他还转动巨型风车的翅膀，

风向标喜欢他，转而寻找

他的影踪——但是这个漫游者已无影无踪！

笑啊，跳啊，晴天的风，

呼啸啊，咆哮啊，雨天的风，

无论东风西风还是南风北风，

每一种风都是我最爱的风。

松树快乐地向他投掷松果，

花儿礼貌地冲他微微颔首，

每一朵浪花都掀起一场珍珠雨，

学校前面的旗帜也迎风招展。

笑啊，跳啊，晴天的风，

呼啸啊，咆哮啊，雨天的风，

无论东风西风还是南风北风，

每一种风都是我最爱的风。

Like Rain It Sounded till It Curved

by Emily Dickinson

Like Rain it sounded till it curved,

And then I knew ’twas Wind—

It walked as wet as any Wave

But swept as dry as sand—

When it had pushed itself away

To some remotest Plain,

A coming as of Hosts was heard

It filled the Wells, it pleased the Pools

It warbled in the Road—

It pulled the spigot from the Hills

And let the Floods abroad—

It loosened acres, lifted seas

The sites of Centres stirred,

Then like Elijah rode away

Upon a Wheel of Cloud.

听起来像雨声，直到它弯曲

[美国] 艾米莉 · 狄金森

听起来像雨声，直到它弯曲，
而后我意识到原来是风——
它走来　犹如潮湿的波浪，
但扫过　仿佛干燥的沙壤——
当它一路呼啸而去，
去到某个偏远的平原，
此起彼伏的风声响起。
它盈满了水井，取悦了湖泊，
它在路上婉转高歌——
它在群山拧开了龙头，
又让洪水肆虐着四方——
它让田野变得松软，又掀起大海的波浪，
它在中部平原上下翻飞，
接着就像伊利亚那样，
乘着祥云飞驰而去。

How Lonesome the Wind Must Feel Nights

by Emily Dickinson

How lonesome the Wind must feel Nights—
When people have put out the Lights
And everything that has an Inn
Closes the shutter and goes in—

How pompous the Wind must feel Noons
Stepping to incorporeal Tunes
Correcting errors of the sky
And clarifying scenery

How mighty the Wind must feel Morns
Encamping on a thousand dawns
Espousing each and spurning all
Then soaring to his Temple Tall—

风在夜晚一定觉得无比孤独

[美国] 艾米莉 · 狄金森

风在夜晚一定觉得无比孤独——
当人们熄灭了所有的灯，
每个可以去客栈歇息的人，
都关上了百叶窗，进入室内——

风在正午一定觉得无比娇傲，
脚踏着无形的旋律，
纠正天空的错误，
还把风景变得澄明。

风在清晨一定觉得无比强大，
在一千个黎明安营扎寨。
拥抱一切又拒绝所有，
而后扶摇直上他高高的庙堂——

Fragment 3: Come, Come Thou Bleak December Wind

by Samuel Taylor Coleridge

Come, come thou bleak December wind,

And blow the dry leaves from the tree!

Flash, like a Love-thought, thro' me, Death

And take a Life that wearies me.

片段之三：来吧，来吧，你那十二月的冷风

[英国] 塞缪尔 · 泰勒 · 柯勒律治

来吧，来吧，你那十二月的冷风，
把干枯的叶子从树上吹落！
刺穿我吧，死亡，像爱的念头一闪而过，
带走这让我疲惫的一生。

The Night Wind

by John Gould Fletcher

Adagio lamentoso

Wind of the night, wind of the long cool shadows,
Wind from the garden gate stealing up the avenue,
Wind caressing my cool pale cheek completely,
All my happiness goes out to you.

Wind flapping aimlessly at my yellow window curtain,
Wind suddenly insisting on your way down to the sea,
Buoyant wind, sobbing wind, wind shuddering and plaintive,
Why come you from beyond through the night's blue mystery?

Wind of my dream, wind of the delicate beauty,
Wind strumming idly at the harp-strings of my

heart:

Wind of the autumn—O melancholy beauty,

Touch me once—one instant—you and I shall never part!

Wind of the night, wind that has fallen silent,

Wind from the dark beyond crying suddenly, eerily,

What terrible news have you shrieked out there in the stillness?

The night is cool and quiet and the wind has crept to sea.

夜晚的风

[美国]约翰·古尔德·弗莱彻

悲伤的慢板

夜晚的风，悠长又阴凉的风，
从花园大门吹来的风沿着林荫道蜿蜒而行，
风尽情抚摸我冰凉苍白的面颊，
我所有的欢愉都向你致敬。

风漫无目的地拍打着我黄色的窗帘，
又突然执意要去往大海的方向，
轻快的风，抽泣的风，颤抖又哀怨的风，
你为何要穿过夜晚那蓝色的神秘？

我梦里的风，纤纤美人般的风，
风悠闲地撩拨着我心中的琴弦：
秋日的风——哦，忧郁的美人，
你只需触碰我一次，哪怕只有一秒，你和我也将永不分离！

夜晚的风，陷入沉默的风，

黑暗里吹来的风忽然开始怪异地哭泣，

你在寂静中尖叫出了什么可怕的消息？

夜色凉爽又静谧，风已悄然飘向大海。

Moon
月亮

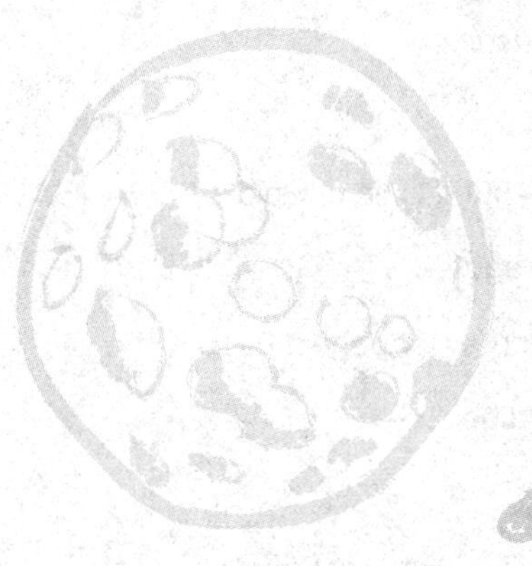

The Moon Was but A Chin of Gold

by Emily Dickinson

The Moon was but a Chin of Gold
A Night or two ago—
And now she turns Her perfect Face
Upon the World below—

Her Forehead is of Amplest Blonde—
Her Cheek—a Beryl hewn—
Her Eye unto the Summer Dew
The likest I have known—

Her Lips of Amber never part—
But what must be the smile
Upon Her Friend she could confer
Were such Her Silver Will—

And what a privilege to be
But the remotest Star—
For Certainty She take Her Way

Beside Your Palace Door—

Her Bonnet is the Firmament—

The Universe—Her Shoe—

The Stars—the Trinkets at Her Belt—

Her Dimities—of Blue—

月亮不过是一个金色的下颚

[美国] 艾米莉 · 狄金森

就在一两个夜晚之前
月亮不过是一个金色的下颚——
现在她转过完美的脸庞
望着下面的世界——

她的前额是最饱和的金色——
她的脸颊——刀削的绿柱石——
我所知道最像夏日露珠的
就是她的眼睛——

她琥珀般的嘴唇从不张开——
但那里一定潜藏着笑容
她所能赠予她朋友的
便是这银色的意志——

最遥远的恒星
有着多么尊贵的特权——
她一定路过了

你殿堂的大门——

苍穹就是她的软帽——
宇宙——她的屐履——
群星——她腰间的挂饰——
蔚蓝色——她的纱袍——

Song of the Moon

by Claude McKay

The moonlight breaks upon the city's domes,
And falls along cemented steel and stone,
Upon the grayness of a million homes,
Lugubrious in unchanging monotone.
Upon the clothes behind the tenement,
That hang like ghosts suspended from the lines,
Linking each flat to each indifferent,
Incongruous and strange the moonlight shines.

There is no magic from your presence here,
Ho, moon, sad moon, tuck up your trailing robe,
Whose silver seems antique and so severe
Against the glow of one electric globe.

Go spill your beauty on the laughing faces
Of happy flowers that bloom a thousand hues,
Waiting on tiptoe in the wilding spaces,
To drink your wine mixed with sweet drafts of dews.

月之歌

[美国] 克劳德 · 麦凯

月光碎在城市的穹顶上，
沿着水泥的钢石纷纷掉落，
落到一百万座房子的晦暗里，
不变的单调与凄凉。
落到廉租公寓后面的衣服上，
它们就像挂在晾衣绳上的鬼魂，
漠然地连接起每一个公寓，
被月光照出突兀怪诞的影子。

你在这里施展不了魔法，
哦，月亮，哀伤的月亮，收起你的曳尾长裙吧，
在地球灯红酒绿的映衬下
你的银辉显得那么古板与严肃。

去把你的美泼洒在欢笑的脸上吧
那些笑脸属于能绽放一千种色彩的花，
它们踮着脚尖在荒野里等待，
等待痛饮你混合了甜蜜露水的美酒。

The Waning Moon

by Percy Bysshe Shelley

And like a dying lady, lean and pale,
Who totters forth, wrapp'd in a gauzy veil,
Out of her chamber, led by the insane
And feeble wanderings of her fading brain,
The moon arose up in the murky East,
A white and shapeless mass.

下弦月

[英国] 珀西 · 比希 · 雪莱

如一位垂死的女子，她瘦削又苍白，
趺趺撞撞，裹着一袭薄纱，
她走出她的闺房，仿佛由疯子领路
脚步踉跄，神思也恍惚，
这月亮从昏暗的东边升起，
白色的一团，没有形状。

To the Moon

by Percy Bysshe Shelley

I

Art thou pale for weariness

Of climbing heaven and gazing on the earth,

Wandering companionless

Among the stars that have a different birth,

And ever changing, like a joyless eye

That finds no object worth its constancy?

II

Thou chosen sister of the Spirit,

That gazes on thee till in thee it pities ...

致月亮

[英国] 珀西 · 比希 · 雪莱

一

你面色苍白，是否因为厌倦了
爬上高空，凝望大地?
在生辰不同的群星之间
孤零零地游荡，
你变幻莫测，就像悲伤的眼睛
找不到任何值得停留的目标?

二

你选择了灵魂做你的姐妹，
她注视着你，直到对你满是怜惜……

The Rose of Midnight

by Vachel Lindsay

The moon is now an opening flower,
The sky a cliff of blue.
The moon is now a silver rose;
Her pollen is the dew.

Her pollen is the mist that swings
Across her face of dreams:
Her pollen is the April rain,
Filling the April streams.

Her pollen is eternal life,
Endless ambrosial foam.
It feeds the swarming stars and fills
Their hearts with honeycomb.

The earth is but a passion-flower
With blood upon his crown.
And what shall fill his failing veins

And lift his head, bowed down?

This cup of peace, this silver rose

Bending with fairy breath

Shall lift that passion-flower, the earth

A million times from Death!

午夜的玫瑰

[美国] 维切尔 · 林赛

月亮此刻是一朵盛开的花，
天空是悬崖上的一抹蓝色。
月亮此刻是一枝银色的玫瑰；
她的花粉就是露水。

她的花粉是浮动的雾气，
拂过她梦中的脸庞：
她的花粉是四月的雨水，
灌溉了四月的溪流。

她的花粉是永恒的生命，
散发着芳香的无尽泡沫。
它滋养了繁星，用蜂房
填满了他们的心房。

大地不过是一朵西番莲
他的皇冠沾满了鲜血。
什么能充盈他日渐干瘪的血脉

让他时而俯首，时而又把头扬?

是这和平的圣杯，是这银色的玫瑰，

她弯下腰来，带着一缕仙气。

她将托起大地这朵西番莲，

无数次地将他从冥府那里举起!

The Crazed Moon

by William Butler Yeats

Crazed through much child-bearing

The moon is staggering in the sky;

Moon-struck by the despairing

Glances of her wandering eye

We grope, and grope in vain,

For children born of her pain.

Children dazed or dead!

When she in all her virginal pride

First trod on the mountain's head

What stir ran through the countryside

Where every foot obeyed her glance!

What manhood led the dance!

Fly-catchers of the moon,

Our hands are blenched, our fingers seem

But slender needles of bone;

Blenched by that malicious dream

They are spread wide that each

May rend what comes in reach.

疯狂的月亮

[爱尔兰] 威廉 · 巴特勒 · 叶芝

因多次怀孕而疯狂，
月亮在天上跌跌撞撞；
那飘忽不定的绝望眼神，
让她饱受创伤。
我们寻觅着，徒劳地寻觅着，
从她的阵痛中降生的孩子们。

孩子们不是痴呆就是死亡！
当她满怀着处女般的骄傲，
首次登上这座山头，
整个村子经历了怎样的轰动，
每个足印都接受她目光的洗礼！
怎样的男子气概引领了这支舞蹈！

月亮上的捕手，
我们的双手开始退缩，我们的手指似乎
不过是骨制的细针；

那个可怕的梦让我们退缩，

五根手指都分开，每一根

都可以撕裂触手可及的东西。

The Moon

by Henry David Thoreau

Time wears her not; she doth his chariot guide;

Mortality below her orb is placed.

—Raleigh

The full-orbed moon with unchanged ray

Mounts up the eastern sky,

Not doomed to these short nights for aye,

But shining steadily.

She does not wane, but my fortune,

Which her rays do not bless,

My wayward path declineth soon,

But she shines not the less.

And if she faintly glimmers here,

And paled is her light,

Yet alway in her proper sphere

She's mistress of the night.

月亮

[美国] 亨利·戴维·梭罗

时间不会磨损她；她是时光战车的驾驶者；

死亡放置在她球形身体的下方。

——纳罗利

满月带着不变的光芒

爬上东方的天空，

她没有陨落在这些短暂的夜晚，

而是持续地照耀四方。

她不会缺损，然而我的命运，

却在她的光芒无法惠及的地方，

我无常的道路很快将走到终点，

但是她的光亮丝毫未减。

就算此时她稍显暗淡，

光芒也苍白了些许，

她也总保持合宜的尺度

因为她是这夜晚的主人。

Phases of the Moon

by Elinor Wylie

Once upon a time I heard

That the flying moon was a Phoenix bird;

Thus she sails through windy skies,

Thus in the willow's arms she lies;

Turn to the East or turn to the West

In many trees she makes her nest.

When she's but a pearly thread

Look among birch leaves overhead;

When she dies in yellow smoke

Look in a thunder-smitten oak;

But in May when the moon is full,

Bright as water and white as wool,

Look for her where she loves to be,

Asleep in a high magnolia tree.

月相

[美国] 埃莉诺 · 怀利

很久以前我曾听说
飞翔的月亮是一只凤凰；
她就这样穿过多风的天空，
她就这样躺在柳树的怀里；
时而朝东，时而朝西
在很多树上搭巢做窝。
当她还是一根珠玉的线条
在头顶的桦树叶间茫然四顾；
当她在黄色的烟雾中死去，
从一棵被雷电击中的橡树上望去；
然而到了五月的月满之时，
她像泉水一样清亮，羊毛一样洁白，
去她钟爱的地方找寻她的芳踪，
她正在一株高高的玉兰树上酣睡。

Water
流水

Spring Pools

by Robert Frost

These pools that, though in forests, still reflect
The total sky almost without defect,
And like the flowers beside them, chill and shiver,
Will like the flowers beside them soon be gone,
And yet not out by any brook or river,
But up by roots to bring dark foliage on.

The trees that have it in their pent-up buds
To darken nature and be summer woods—
Let them think twice before they use their powers
To blot out and drink up and sweep away
These flowery waters and these watery flowers
From snow that melted only yesterday.

春日的池塘

[美国] 罗伯特 · 弗罗斯特

这些池塘，虽然身处森林，
仍然几近完美地映照整个天空，
它们像水边的花朵，瑟瑟颤抖，
也像水边的花朵，转瞬即逝，
但它们不是被溪流或河水吞噬，
而是被树根吸收，激发深色的叶片。

树木把水分贮存在它们幽闭的新芽中
把自然染成深色，化为夏天的树林——
让树木在施展威力之前，
把这片花样的池水和这些水边的花朵
榨干、喝光、摧毁之前，再三思忖，
要知道它们昨天才刚由冰雪消融而来。

To the River

by Edgar Allan Poe

Fair river! in thy bright, clear flow
Of crystal, wandering water,
Thou art an emblem of the glow
Of beauty—the unhidden heart—
The playful maziness of art
In old Alberto's daughter;

But when within thy wave she looks—
Which glistens then, and trembles—
Why, then, the prettiest of brooks
Her worshipper resembles;
For in my heart, as in thy stream,
Her image deeply lies—
His heart which trembles at the beam
Of her soul-searching eyes.

致河流

[美国] 埃德加·爱伦·坡

美丽的河流！你水晶般的流水
明媚又清澈地流动，
你是美——那光彩夺目的徽章，
你是那昭然若揭的心，
你是老阿尔贝托的爱女身上
那座顽皮的艺术迷宫。

然而当她从你的浪花里向外张望——
河面波光粼粼、微微颤动——
她的爱慕者为何
与最迷人的那条溪流相仿；
因为在我的心里，就像在你的水中，
她的形象深深地映入——
她摄人魂魄的双眼所绽放的光芒
让他的心也跟着悸动。

The Lake

by Edgar Allan Poe

In spring of youth it was my lot
To haunt of the wide world a spot
The which I could not love the less—
So lovely was the loneliness
Of a wild lake, with black rock bound,
And the tall pines that towered around.

But when the Night had thrown her pall
Upon that spot, as upon all,
And the mystic wind went by
Murmuring in melody—
Then—ah then I would awake
To the terror of the lone lake

Yet that terror was not fright,
But a tremulous delight—
A feeling not the jewelled mine
Could teach or bribe me to define—

Nor Love—although the Love were thine.

Death was in that poisonous wave,

And in its gulf a fitting grave

For him who thence could solace bring

To his lone imagining—

Whose solitary soul could make

An Eden of that dim lake.

湖

[美国] 埃德加 · 爱伦 · 坡

我年少之时于冥冥之中，
常常造访这广袤天地的一角。
我对它的爱深彻入骨——
那野湖的寂寞如此可爱，
湖畔布满黑色的岩石，
还有高耸入云的松树。

然而当夜幕降临，
那个地方与世界一并被笼罩，
当神秘的风从耳边吹过，
浅吟低唱着它的旋律——
那时——啊，那时我才醒悟，
意识到那孤湖的阴森可怖。

不过那可怖不是一种惊吓，
而是一种战栗的快乐——
那样的感觉，即便用珠宝的矿藏
也不能引导或贿赂我给出定义——

连爱也不能——哪怕那爱来自你。

死亡就在那有毒的水波里，

沟壑处有一座适合他的坟墓。

他能从那里

给自己孤独的想象带来慰藉——

他寂寞的灵魂能够把

那暗淡的湖变为伊甸园。

The Lake

by James Stephens

He could see the little lake
Cuddled on a mountain's arm,
And the rushes were a'shake,
On the margin of the lake.

And the gloom of evening threw
On the surface of the lake,
Just a shadow on the blue
Where the night came creeping through.

There was silence all around,
Not a whisper stirred the lake,
And the trees made not a sound
Standing silent in the ground.

Then a moon of beauty swept
One slim finger on the lake,
And the glory of it crept

Past the lilies where they slept,

And just where a lily flung
Its broad flag upon the lake
Was a dead face pale and young
And the wet hair spread and swung;

And the moon beamed mild and dim
On that dead face in the lake,
Then it grew fierce, wide and grim,
And a mad moon glared at Him.

湖

[爱尔兰] 詹姆斯 · 史蒂芬斯

他能看到小小的湖
依偎在高山的怀里，
灯芯草微微摇曳着，
在湖边的空地。

傍晚的昏暗投在
湖面之上，
如同投在蓝色上的一片阴影
夜就从那里悄悄潜入。

周遭静悄悄的，
连搅动湖水的低语也没有，
树林也无声
沉默地伫立于大地。

接着，一轮明月
用一根纤细的手指拂过湖面，
它的光辉偷偷地掠过

百合们沉睡的地方，

其中一朵
把它硕大的花瓣探向湖水。
那里有一张死去的脸庞，苍白又年轻，
他的湿发披散开来，随波荡漾；

月光柔和而暗淡
映照在湖里死者的脸上，
而后那张脸变得凶残、阔大又冷酷，
发疯的月亮直直地盯着他不放。

Season

四季

From Spring Days to Winter

by Oscar Wilde

In the glad springtime when leaves were green,
O merrily the throstle sings!
I sought, amid the tangled sheen,
Love whom mine eyes had never seen,
O the glad dove has golden wings!

Between the blossoms red and white,
O merrily the throstle sings!
My love first came into my sight,
O perfect vision of delight,
O the glad dove has golden wings!

The yellow apples glowed like fire,
O merrily the throstle sings!
O Love too great for lip or lyre,
Blown rose of love and of desire,
O the glad dove has golden wings!
But now with snow the tree is grey,

Ah, sadly now the throstle sings!

My love is dead: ah! well-a-day,

See at her silent feet I lay

A dove with broken wings!

Ah, Love! ah, Love! that thou wert slain—

Fond Dove, fond Dove return again!

从春日到寒冬

[爱尔兰] 奥斯卡 · 王尔德

明媚的春光里树叶焕发新绿，
哦，画眉愉快地歌唱！
我在纷乱的光影中寻找，
我的双眼不曾见过的爱人，
哦，欢乐的鸽子有一对金色的翅膀！

在争奇斗艳的朱红和雪白之间，
哦，画眉愉快地歌唱！
我的爱人第一次映入眼帘，
哦，带来喜悦的完美景象，
哦，欢乐的鸽子有一对金色的翅膀！

金黄的苹果像火焰一样发光，
哦，画眉愉快地歌唱！
哦，爱太伟大了，无法用言语或竖琴描述，
爱情与欲望的玫瑰已经绽放，
哦，欢乐的鸽子有一对金色的翅膀！

然而现在树木凋零、雪花飞扬，

啊，画眉如今悲伤地歌唱！

我的爱人已死：啊！呜呼哀哉，

看呵，在她一动不动的脚旁，

我放了一只折翅的鸽子！

啊，我的爱人！啊，我的爱情！你被杀死

心爱的鸽子，起死回生吧，心爱的鸽子！

Azure and Gold

by Amy Lowell

April had covered the hills
With flickering yellows and reds,
The sparkle and coolness of snow
Was blown from the mountain beds.

Across a deep-sunken stream
The pink of blossoming trees,
And from windless appleblooms
The humming of many bees.

The air was of rose and gold
Arabesqued with the song of birds
Who, swinging unseen under leaves,
Made music more eager than words.

Of a sudden, aslant the road,
A brightness to dazzle and stun,
A glint of the bluest blue,

A flash from a sapphire sun.

Blue-birds so blue, 't was a dream,
An impossible, unconceived hue,
The high sky of summer dropped down
Some rapturous ocean to woo.

Such a colour, such infinite light!
The heart of a fabulous gem,
Many-faceted, brilliant and rare.
Centre Stone of the earth's diadem!

Centre Stone of the Crown of the World,
"Sincerity" graved on your youth!
And your eyes hold the blue-bird flash,
The sapphire shaft, which is truth.

蓝色和金色

[美国] 艾米 · 洛威尔

四月把山丘覆盖上了
明灭的黄色与红色，
晶莹又凉爽的雪
从山涧的河床被吹落。

一条深邃的小溪流经
开满粉色花朵的树林，
从无风的苹果花丛
传来群蜂的嗡嗡叫声。

空气中弥漫着玫瑰与金黄
与鸟鸣汇合成阿拉伯的舞曲。
是谁，在树叶下悄悄地摇摆，
让那音乐比言辞更加热烈。

忽然，道路急转直下，
耀眼的光芒倾泻而下，
那是一片最蓝的蓝色，

是蓝宝石般的太阳发出的光芒。

蓝鸟如此地蓝，如梦境一般，
一种不可思议又浑然天成的色调，
仿佛夏日的高空降下了
一汪狂热的海水来求爱。

这样的色彩，这样无限的光！
像一颗神奇宝石的心脏，
多面、璀璨又稀有。
大地王冠上的主钻！

世界王冠上的主钻，
“真诚”刻在你的青春之上！
你的双眼闪烁着蓝鸟的光，
一束蓝宝石般的光，名为真相。

The Enkindled Spring

by David Herbert Lawrence

This spring as it comes bursts up in bonfires green,
Wild puffing of emerald trees, and flame-filled bushes,
Thorn-blossom lifting in wreaths of smoke between
Where the wood fumes up and the watery, flickering
rushes.

I am amazed at this spring, this conflagration
Of green fires lit on the soil of the earth, this blaze
Of growing, and sparks that puff in wild gyration,
Faces of people streaming across my gaze.

And I, what fountain of fire am I among
This leaping combustion of spring? My spirit is tossed
About like a shadow buffeted in the throng
Of flames, a shadow that's gone astray, and is lost.

被点燃的春天

[英国]戴维 · 赫伯特 · 劳伦斯

春天来了，在篝火中迸发绿色，

翠绿的树林和燃烧的灌木洋溢狂野的气息，

荆棘花在烟雾的萦绕中绽放

在树林起烟和水光潋滟的地方。

春天令我感到如此神奇，

这场绿色的大火席卷了大地，

万物生长的火焰和疯狂旋转的火花，

人们匆匆而过的脸庞接受着我的注目礼。

而我，在春天跳跃的火苗中。

这是怎样的火之喷泉？我的精神

摇来荡去，像一个影子在火海中起伏，

这影子误入了歧途，就此迷失。

A Memory of June

by Claude McKay

When June comes dancing o'er the death of May,
With scarlet roses tinting her green breast,
And mating thrushes ushering in her day,
And Earth on tiptoe for her golden guest,

I always see the evening when we met—
The first of June baptized in tender rain—-
And walked home through the wide streets, gleaming wet,
Arms locked, our warm flesh pulsing with love's pain.

I always see the cheerful little room,
And in the corner, fresh and white, the bed,
Sweet scented with a delicate perfume,
Wherein for one night only we were wed;

Where in the starlit stillness we lay mute,

And heard the whispering showers all night long,
And your brown burning body was a lute
Whereon my passion played his fevered song.

When June comes dancing o'er the death of May,
With scarlet roses staining her fair feet,
My soul takes leave of me to sing all day
A love so fugitive and so complete.

六月的回忆

[美国] 克劳德 · 麦凯

六月款款而来，伴随着五月的逝去，
猩红的玫瑰浸润着她绿色的胸脯，
交配的画眉迎来了属于她的一天，
大地踮起脚尖迎接她金色的客人。

我总是看到我们相遇的那个夜晚——
六月的第一天在温柔的细雨中受洗——
穿过宽阔的街道步行回家，浑身湿透，
紧抱双臂，我们温暖的血肉随着爱的苦痛而跳动。

我总是看到那个让人愉悦的小小房间，
角落里，那清新洁白的，是我们的床，
它散发着淡雅又甜蜜的芳香，
在那里，我们只度过了一晚婚期；

寂静的星空下我们沉默地躺着，
听着如泣如诉的雨下了一夜，
你那晒成棕色的身体是一把琉特琴

我的激情在那上面奏出热烈的歌。

六月款款而来，伴随着五月的逝去，
猩红的玫瑰浸染着她美丽的双脚，
我的灵魂离我而去，整日吟唱，
吟唱那爱情如此短暂又如此完整。

To Winter

by Claude McKay

Stay, season of calm love and soulful snows!
There is a subtle sweetness in the sun,
The ripples on the stream's breast gaily run,
The wind more boisterously by me blows,
And each succeeding day now longer grows.
The birds a gladder music have begun,
The squirrel, full of mischief and of fun,
From maples' topmost branch the brown twig throws.
I read these pregnant signs, know what they mean:
I know that thou art making ready to go.
Oh stay! I fled a land where fields are green
Always, and palms wave gently to and fro,
And winds are balmy, blue brooks ever sheen,
To ease my heart of its impassioned woe.

致冬天

[美国]克劳德·麦凯

留下来，平静的爱和深情的雪之季节！
阳光里有一种微妙的甜蜜，
溪流涌起的涟漪欢快地流淌着，
风从我身边嬉笑着吹过，
接下来的每一个白天变得愈来愈长。
鸟儿们奏起更加欢快的乐曲，
松鼠，忙着玩耍和恶作剧，
从枫树最高处的枝条扔出棕色的树枝。
我读着这些饱含意味的迹象，明白了它们的寓意：
我知道你已准备离去。
哦，留下来吧！我逃离了一片常绿的田野
那里的棕榈轻轻地来回挥舞，
那里的风是温和的，那蓝色的溪流永远波光闪烁，
抚慰我内心不绝的伤痛。

Song: Spring

by William Shakespeare

(from *Love's Labours Lost*)

When daisies pied and violets blue
And lady-smocks all silver-white
And cuckoo-buds of yellow hue
Do paint the meadows with delight,
The cuckoo then, on every tree,
Mocks married men; for thus sings he,
Cuckoo;
Cuckoo, cuckoo: Oh word of fear,
Unpleasing to a married ear!

When shepherds pipe on oaten straws,
And merry larks are plowmen's clocks,
When turtles tread, and rooks, and daws,
And maidens bleach their summer smocks,
The cuckoo then, on every tree,
Mocks married men; for thus sings he,

Cuckoo;

Cuckoo, cuckoo: Oh word of fear,

Unpleasing to a married ear!

歌：春天

[英国]威廉·莎士比亚

（选自《爱的徒劳》）

当杂色的雏菊与蓝色的罗兰绽放，
当女子身穿银白的衣裳，
当杜鹃吐露黄色的花蕾，
用欢愉为草地着色上妆，
布谷鸟在每棵树上逗留，
取笑已婚的男子；他这样唱道，
布谷；
布谷，布谷：哦，可怕的声音，
对于已婚人士真是刺耳！

当牧童吹起了燕麦秆做的笛子，
当快乐的云雀叫醒了犁地的农夫，
当斑鸠交合，白嘴鸭和穴鸟也纷纷寻伴，
当少女们浣洗她们夏日的长衫，
布谷鸟在每棵树上逗留，
取笑已婚的男子；他这样唱道，

布谷；

布谷，布谷：哦，可怕的声音，

对于已婚人士真是刺耳！

Sonnet 18: Shall I Compare Thee to A Summer's Day?

by William Shakespeare

Shall I compare thee to a summer's day?
Thou art more lovely and more temperate.
Rough winds do shake the darling buds of May,
And summer's lease hath all too short a date.
Sometime too hot the eye of heaven shines,
And often is his gold complexion dimmed;
And every fair from fair sometime declines,
By chance, or nature's changing course, untrimmed;
But thy eternal summer shall not fade,
Nor lose possession of that fair thou ow'st,
Nor shall death brag thou wand'rest in his shade,
When in eternal lines to Time thou grow'st.
So long as men can breathe, or eyes can see,
So long lives this, and this gives life to thee.

十四行诗 18：我应否把你比作夏日的一天？

[英国] 威廉 · 莎士比亚

我应否把你比作夏日的一天？
你比之更加可爱也更加温婉。
狂风会肆虐五月娇嫩的蓓蕾，
夏日出赁的租期又太过短暂。
天空的眼睛有时照射得过于炙热，
他金色的肌肤又常常转瞬暗淡；
没有谁能够青春永驻，
无不被命运或无常的天道摧残；
然而你那永恒的夏日不会褪色，
也不会失去你拥有的美丽容颜，
死神也不敢夸口你在他的阴影下游荡，
当你在永恒的诗句里与时间同往。
只要人类尚有气息，双目尚能观看，
这首诗就将长存，赐予你生命无限。

To See the Summer Sky

by Emily Dickinson

To see the Summer Sky
Is Poetry, though never in a Book it lie—
True Poems flee—

凝望夏日的天空

[美国] 艾米莉 · 狄金森

凝望夏日的天空

仿佛阅读一首诗，尽管它从不躺在书里——

真正的诗从书里逃离——

Autumn Fires

by Robert Louis Stevenson

In the other gardens
And all up the vale,
From the autumn bonfires
See the smoke trail!

Pleasant summer over
And all the summer flowers,
The red fire blazes,
The grey smoke towers.

Sing a song of seasons!
Something bright in all!
Flowers in the summer,
Fires in the fall!

秋日的火

[英国] 罗伯特 · 路易斯 · 史蒂文森

飘入别人的花园
弥漫所有的溪谷，
从那秋日的篝火
看炊烟袅袅升起！

快乐的夏天已结束
夏日的花朵也落幕，
红色的篝火在燃烧，
灰色的烟雾也腾起。

唱一首四季的歌吧！
它们各有各的精彩！
夏天有盛放的花朵，
秋天有燃烧的篝火！

The Cocoon

by Robert Frost

As far as I can see this autumn haze
That spreading in the evening air both way,
Makes the new moon look anything but new,
And pours the elm-tree meadow full of blue,
Is all the smoke from one poor house alone
With but one chimney it can call its own;
So close it will not light an early light,
Keeping its life so close and out of sign
No one for hours has set a foot outdoors
So much as to take care of evening chores.
The inmates may be lonely women-folk.
I want to tell them that with all this smoke
They prudently are spinning their cocoon
And anchoring it to an earth and moon
From which no winter gale can hope to blow it—
Spinning their own cocoon did they but know it.

茧

[美国] 罗伯特 · 弗罗斯特

极目远眺，我能看到秋日的薄雾
以两种方式，弥漫在黄昏的空气中，
让新月看起来那么陈旧，
把长着榆树的草地蒙上一层蓝烟，
是从一座孤寂的破旧小屋里升起的炊烟，
那小屋只拥有一根烟囱；
它孤寂到不愿意早早点灯，
过着寂寥又远离尘嚣的生活
数个小时，也无一人出门，
哪怕只是料理一下傍晚的杂务。
屋内也许住着几个孤独的女人。
我想告诉她们，她们正用这炊烟
小心地编织着自己的茧，
把它牢系在大地和月亮之间。
就连冬日的狂风也别指望把它吹散——
她们清楚她们在编织着自己的茧。

Plant
草木

In the Forest

by Oscar Wilde

Out of the mid-wood's twilight
Into the meadow's dawn,
Ivory limbed and brown-eyed,
Flashes my Faun!

He skips through the copses singing,
And his shadow dances along,
And I know not which I should follow,
Shadow or song!

O Hunter, snare me his shadow!
O Nightingale, catch me his strain!
Else moonstruck with music and madness
I track him in vain!

森林里

[爱尔兰] 奥斯卡 · 王尔德

告别密林的暮光，
迎来牧场的黎明，
象牙色的四肢和棕色的眼睛，
我的牧神闪现身影！

他边唱边跃过灌木丛，
他的影子也随之起舞，
我不知该追随哪一个，
他的影子还是歌声！

哦猎人，帮我诱捕他的影子！
哦夜莺，替我抓住他的歌声！
否则，被音乐和疯魔撕扯的我
对他的追踪将一无所获。

The Sound of Trees

by Robert Frost

I wonder about the trees.
Why do we wish to bear
Forever the noise of these
More than another noise
So close to our dwelling place?
We suffer them by the day
Till we lose all measure of pace,
And fixity in our joys,
And acquire a listening air.
They are that that talks of going
But never gets away;
And that talks no less for knowing,
As it grows wiser and older,
That now it means to stay.
My feet tug at the floor
And my head sways to my shoulder
Sometimes when I watch trees sway,
From the window or the door.

I shall set forth for somewhere,
I shall make the reckless choice
Some day when they are in voice
And tossing so as to scare
The white clouds over them on.
I shall have less to say,
But I shall be gone.

树木的声音

[美国] 罗伯特 · 弗罗斯特

树木让我陷入沉思。
为何我们愿意
永远忍受这些噪音,
却拒斥其他噪音,
更何况树木与我们的居所还近在咫尺?
我们日日饱受它们的折磨
直至失去对所有节奏的丈量,
失去我们日常的愉悦,
只换来一种聆听的气氛。
它们一直在谈论离开
但从未离开半步;
随着智慧和年龄日渐增长,
越发高谈要开阔眼界,
然而如今却意图留下。
我在地板上拖着步子,
我的脑袋转向肩膀的一侧。
这些时候我望向窗外或门外,
看着树木迎风摆动。

我要出发去某个地方，

我要做出冲动的选择。

总有一天，当树木谈起这些，

猛烈摇晃，试图吓退

它们头顶飘浮的白云。

我不会学它们那样饶舌，

但是我会立刻动身。

The Forest Reverie

by Edgar Allan Poe

'Tis said that when
The hands of men
Tamed this primeval wood,
And hoary trees with groans of woe,
Like warriors by an unknown foe,
Were in their strength subdued,
The virgin Earth Gave instant birth
To springs that ne'er did flow.
That in the sun Did rivulets run,
And all around rare flowers did blow
The wild rose pale Perfumed the gale
And the queenly lily adown the dale
(Whom the sun and the dew
And the winds did woo),
With the gourd and the grape luxuriant grew.

So when in tears
The love of years

Is wasted like the snow,
And the fine fibrils of its life
By the rude wrong of instant strife
Are broken at a blow
Within the heart
Do springs upstart
Of which it doth now know,
And strange, sweet dreams,
Like silent streams
That from new fountains overflow,
With the earlier tide
Of rivers glide
Deep in the heart whose hope has died—
Quenching the fires its ashes hide,—
Its ashes, whence will spring and grow
Sweet flowers, ere long,
The rare and radiant flowers of song!

森林遐想

[美国] 埃德加 · 爱伦 · 坡

据说当

人类的手

驯服了这片原始森林，

发出悲鸣的老树，

就像勇士面对着未知的敌人，

遭遇重创，

处女地立刻孕育出

那从不流动的泉水。

虽然在阳光的照射下那溪流的确涌动，

周围那罕见的花朵也的确盛放，

野玫瑰在狂风中散发着清香，

还有山谷中的女王百合

（她是阳光、露水和风求爱的对象），

还有葫芦和葡萄也竞相疯长。

所以当它落泪，

为这经年的爱，

不过荒废如白雪，

组成它生命的细小纤维
被暴力转瞬摧毁，
轰然倒塌。
从它的心里
突然涌出泉水。
如今它终于醒悟，
诡谲又甜蜜的梦啊，
就像安静的溪流
从新的泉眼溢出，
随着原始河流的涌动
而流动。
内心深处的希望已经破灭——
熄灭了火焰，又藏起了灰烬——
然而正是灰烬让万物复苏，
不久便会长出甜美的花朵，
罕见而绚烂的花朵，仿佛一首歌！

On A Tree Fallen across the Road

by Robert Frost

(To hear us talk)

The tree the tempest with a crash of wood
Throws down in front of us is not bar
Our passage to our journey's end for good,
But just to ask us who we think we are

Insisting always on our own way so.
She likes to halt us in our runner tracks,
And make us get down in a foot of snow
Debating what to do without an ax.

And yet she knows obstruction is in vain:
We will not be put off the final goal
We have it hidden in us to attain,
Not though we have to seize earth by the pole

And, tired of aimless circling in one place,
Steer straight off after something into space.

倒在路上的一棵树

[美国] 罗伯特 · 弗罗斯特

（听到我们交谈）

狂风暴雨击倒了此树，
横亘眼前的并不是围栏。
我们的旅程就此告终，
却只想自问我们究竟是谁。

我们一直坚持走自己的道路。
但她喜欢在赛道上阻挠我们，
让我们陷入一英尺深的雪中，
手无寸铁，争论该何去何从。

然而她明白阻挠注定徒劳：
我们不会放弃最后的目标，
我们暗藏必胜的决心，
尽管并非要征服地球的极点。

而后，我们厌倦了在原地盲目兜圈，
面对拦路虎，我们决定另辟蹊径。

Le Jardin

by Oscar Wilde

The lily's withered chalice falls
Around its rod of dusty gold,
And from the beech-trees on the wold
The last wood-pigeon coos and calls.

The gaudy leonine sunflower
Hangs black and barren on its stalk,
And down the windy garden walk
The dead leaves scatter, hour by hour.

Pale privet-petals white as milk
Are blown into a snowy mass:
The roses lie upon the grass
Like little shreds of crimson silk.

花园

[爱尔兰] 奥斯卡 · 王尔德

百合枯萎的圣杯凋落
在它蒙尘的金杖周围，
在荒野的山毛榉树上，
最后的斑鸠发出咕咕鸣叫。

狮子般花哨又张扬的向日葵
挂在茎秆上，贫瘠又乌黑，
沿着起风的花园小径，
时间流逝，枯叶四处散落。

女贞的花瓣像牛奶一样洁白，
蓬松得仿佛一团雪球；
玫瑰花则躺在草地上，
仿佛被撕成了细小碎片的红绸。

The Tree of Scarlet Berries

by Amy Lowell

The rain gullies the garden paths
And tinkles on the broad sides of grass blades.
A tree, at the end of my arm, is hazy with mist.
Even so, I can see that it has red berries,
A scarlet fruit,
Filmed over with moisture.
It seems as though the rain,
Dripping from it,
Should be tinged with colour.
I desire the berries,
But, in the mist, I only scratch my hand on the thorns.
Probably, too, they are bitter.

缀满鲜红浆果的树

[美国] 艾米 · 洛威尔

雨水冲刷着花园的小路
打在草丛的阔叶上叮咚作响。
我手臂尽头的一棵树，在雾气中氤氲。
即便这样，我仍能看到它结了红色的浆果，
一种鲜红的水果，
外皮湿漉漉的。
似乎从它身上
滴落的雨水，
也应该染上颜色。
我想要这些浆果，
然而，雾气中，我只是用手摩挲了一下它们的尖刺。
或许，它们也是苦涩的。

Oh Shadow on the Grass

by Emily Dickinson

Oh Shadow on the Grass,
Art thou a Step or not?
Go make thee fair my Candidate
My nominated Heart—
Oh Shadow on the Grass
While I delay to guess
Some other thou wilt consecrate—
Oh Unelected Face—

哦，草地上的影子

[美国]艾米莉·狄金森

哦，草地上的影子
你是不是一个脚印？
去做我理想的候选人吧
我的心已被提名——
哦，草地上的影子
趁我迟迟未做猜测
你会另寻他方神圣——
哦，落选的脸孔——

Animal
动物

Fireflies in the Garden

by Robert Frost

Here come real stars to fill the upper skies,

And here on earth come emulating flies,

That though they never equal stars in size,

(And they were never really stars at heart)

Achieve at times a very star-like start.

Only, of course, they can't sustain the part.

花园里的萤火虫

[美国] 罗伯特 · 弗罗斯特

真正的星星出来了，布满头顶的夜空，

地上的萤火虫出来了，模仿着星星，

尽管在尺寸上它们无法媲美星星，

（也从未有人真的把它们视作星星）

却时常开启繁星般辉煌的序曲。

只不过，当然了，它们的璀璨并不能持续。

Butterfly

by David Herbert Lawrence

Butterfly, the wind blows sea-ward,
strong beyond the garden-wall!
Butterfly, why do you settle on my
shoe, and sip the dirt on my shoe,
Lifting your veined wings, lifting them?
big white butterfly!

Already it is October, and the wind
blows strong to the sea
from the hills where snow must have
fallen, the wind is polished with
snow.
Here in the garden, with red
geraniums, it is warm, it is warm
but the wind blows strong to sea-ward,
white butterfly, content on my shoe!

Will you go, will you go from my warm

house?
Will you climb on your big soft wings,
black-dotted,
as up an invisible rainbow, an arch
till the wind slides you sheer from the
arch-crest
and in a strange level fluttering you go
out to sea-ward, white speck!

蝴蝶

[英国]戴维·赫伯特·劳伦斯

蝴蝶，风吹向大海，
狂风一直吹过花园的围墙！
蝴蝶，你为何停在我的鞋子上，
还在我的鞋子上啜饮泥土，
扬起你的脉翅，扬起它们？
大大的白色蝴蝶！

已经是十月了，狂风
吹向大海
从注定落满了白雪的山丘吹过，
连风也被雪花装点。
这里的花园开满红色的天竺葵，很暖很暖
但是狂风一直吹向大海，
白色的蝴蝶，为能栖息在我的鞋子上满足！

你会离开吗，你会从我温暖的家园
离开吗？
你会爬上你硕大柔软的翅膀吗？

那双布满黑色斑点的翅膀，

就像爬上一弯看不见的拱形彩虹，

直到风使你从拱顶滑落。

你以奇特的角度震颤着翅膀，

飞向大海，最后化为小小的白点！

Homing Swallows

by Claude McKay

Swift swallows sailing from the Spanish main,
O rain-birds racing merrily away
From hill-tops parched with heat and sultry plain
Of wilting plants and fainting flowers, say—

When at the noon-hour from the chapel school
The children dash and scamper down the dale,
Scornful of teacher's rod and binding rule
Forever broken and without avail.

Do they still stop beneath the giant tree
To gather locusts in their childish greed,
And chuckle when they break the pods to see
The golden powder clustered round the seed?

归家的燕子

[美国]克劳德·麦凯

从西班牙大陆跨海而来的雨燕，
哦，雨中的鸟儿快乐地飞远
或许，它们来自被高温炙烤的炎热山顶
和遍布枯萎植被与凋谢花朵的闷热平原——

正午时分，孩子们从教会学校出来
沿着山谷一路奔跑嬉闹，
嘴里嘲笑着老师的棍棒和规则。
那套陈词滥调已被永远打破，不再生效。

他们是否还在大树下面逗留，
怀着孩子的贪婪收集着蝗虫？
他们是否还会发出咯咯的笑声，
当剥开豆荚　看到种子周围洒满的金色粉末？

To A Squirrel at Kyle-Na-No

by William Butler Yeats

Come play with me;

Why should you run

Through the shaking tree

As though I'd a gun

To strike you dead?

When all I would do

Is to scratch your head

And let you go.

致凯尔奈诺的一只松鼠

[爱尔兰] 威廉 · 巴特勒 · 叶芝

过来和我一起玩儿;

你为什么要逃走

穿过摇摇晃晃的树

仿佛我带着枪

要把你一枪击中?

我打算做的

不过是挠挠你的头

然后把你放走。

Cat's Dream

by Pablo Neruda

How neatly a cat sleeps,
Sleeps with its paws and its posture,
Sleeps with its wicked claws,
And with its unfeeling blood,
Sleeps with ALL the rings a series
Of burnt circles which have formed
The odd geology of its sand-colored tail.

I should like to sleep like a cat,
With all the fur of time,
With a tongue rough as flint,
With the dry sex of fire and
After speaking to no one,
Stretch myself over the world,
Over roofs and landscapes,
With a passionate desire
To hunt the rats in my dreams.

I have seen how the cat asleep
Would undulate, how the night flowed
Through it like dark water and at times,
It was going to fall or possibly
Plunge into the bare deserted snowdrifts.

Sometimes it grew so much in sleep
Like a tiger's great-grandfather,
And would leap in the darkness over
Rooftops, clouds and volcanoes.

Sleep, sleep cat of the night with
Episcopal ceremony and your stone-carved
moustache.
Take care of all our dreams
Control the obscurity
Of our slumbering prowess
With your relentless HEART
And the great ruff of your tail.

猫咪的梦

[智利] 巴勃罗 · 聂鲁达

猫咪睡着的样子多么得体，
爪子和姿态都如此绝妙，
它调皮的爪子与它同睡，
连同那副没心没肺的样子，
和所有的环形共眠。
那一串烧焦的圆圈
组成了它沙色尾巴的奇特曲线。

我要像猫咪那样睡觉，
披着时间的长毛，
舌头如燧石般粗糙，
性爱如烈火般干燥，
不与任何人交谈，
让自己尽情舒展，
越过世界，越过那些屋顶和风景线，
怀着澎湃的欲望
去梦里把老鼠寻找。

我已经目睹了猫咪的睡姿，
身体怎样起伏，夜晚如何流逝，
像幽暗的水流经它，有时
它会掉落或可能陷入
光秃秃的荒凉雪丘。

有时它在梦里无限膨胀，
胀得像老虎的曾祖父，
这时它会翻过屋顶、云层和火山，
纵身跃入黑暗。

睡吧，睡吧，夜晚的猫咪
与主教的仪式和你石刻的胡须同睡。
照看好我们的梦境，
把握好那种安宁，
那是我们沉睡的非凡才能。
以你的没心没肺
和你尾巴的美妙环形。

The White Horse

by David Herbert Lawrence

The youth walks up to the white horse, to put its halter on
and the horse looks at him in silence.
They are so silent, they are in another world.

白马

[英国] 戴维 · 赫伯特 · 劳伦斯

年轻人走向白马，给它套上笼头，

马沉默地看着他。

他们如此沉默，仿佛身处另一个时空。

City
城市

Symphony in Yellow

by Oscar Wilde

An omnibus across the bridge
Crawls like a yellow butterfly
And, here and there, a passer-by
Shows like a little restless midge.

Big barges full of yellow hay
Are moored against the shadowy wharf,
And, like a yellow silken scarf,
The thick fog hangs along the quay.

The yellow leaves begin to fade
And flutter from the Temple elms,
And at my feet the pale green Thames
Lies like a rod of rippled jade.

黄色交响乐

[爱尔兰] 奥斯卡 · 王尔德

一辆正在过桥的公共马车
如一只黄色蝴蝶缓缓爬行。
零零散散，时有行人出现，
像只焦躁不安的小小蠓虫。

大型驳船满载黄色干草
它们在阴凉的码头停靠。
浓雾仿佛一条黄色的丝巾，
在码头上空萦绕。

黄色树叶渐次枯萎凋零，
自教堂的榆树纷纷飘落。
我脚边淡绿的泰晤士河
如一根泛着涟漪的翡翠。

Dawn in New York

by Claude McKay

The Dawn! The Dawn! The crimson-tinted, comes
Out of the low still skies, over the hills,
Manhattan's roofs and spires and cheerless domes!
The Dawn! My spirit to its spirit thrills.
Almost the mighty city is asleep,
No pushing crowd, no tramping, tramping feet.
But here and there a few cars groaning creep
Along, above, and underneath the street,
Bearing their strangely-ghostly burdens by,
The women and the men of garish nights,
Their eyes wine-weakened and their clothes awry,
Grotesques beneath the strong electric lights.
The shadows wane. The Dawn comes to New York.
And I go darkly-rebel to my work.

纽约的黎明

[美国] 克劳德 · 麦凯

黎明！黎明！绯红的颜色，
自平静的低空蔓延开来，越过了山丘，
越过了曼哈顿的平顶、尖顶和沉闷的圆顶！
黎明！我的心灵与之琴瑟和鸣。
这个偌大的城市几乎仍在酣睡，
没有推搡的人群，没有踩踏的脚步。
但时不时便有几辆车呻吟着爬过
从街道的上方或街道的下方，
承受着诡异如幽灵般的重负，
灯红酒绿下的男男女女，
因醉酒而双眼迷离，衣冠也不够整齐，
在刺目路灯的照射下显得光怪陆离。
阴影逐渐消退。黎明来到了纽约。
我出门上班，心里满是黑暗的叛逆。

A Little Road Not Made of Man

by Emily Dickinson

A little road not made of man,
Enabled of the eye,
Accessible to thill of bee,
Or cart of butterfly.

If town it have, beyond itself,
'T is that I cannot say;
I only sigh,— no vehicle
Bears me along that way.

一条并非人造的小路

[美国] 艾米莉 · 狄金森

一条并非人造的小路，

眼睛却有幸看见，

蜜蜂可以在路上驱车，

蝴蝶的马车也可以通过。

小路的尽头是否通向城镇，

我无从把握；

我只能叹气，因为没有交通工具

载着我走向那里。

Subway Wind

by Claude McKay

Far down, down through the city's great, gaunt gut,
The gray train rushing bears the weary wind;
In the packed cars the fans the crowd's breath cut,
Leaving the sick and heavy air behind.
And pale-cheeked children seek the upper door
To give their summer jackets to the breeze;
Their laugh is swallowed in the deafening roar
Of captive wind that moans for fields and seas;
Seas cooling warm where native schooners drift
Through sleepy waters, while gulls wheel and sweep,
Waiting for windy waves the keels to lift
Lightly among the islands of the deep;
Islands of lofty palm trees blooming white
That lend their perfume to the tropic sea,
Where fields lie idle in the dew drenched night,
And the Trades float above them fresh and free.

地铁的风

[美国] 克劳德·麦凯

远远地，穿过城市巨大而憔悴的内脏，
裹挟着疲倦的风，灰色的地铁疾驰而过；
在拥挤的车厢里，风扇截断人群的呼吸，
把污浊又沉重的空气抛在身后。
脸色苍白的孩子们寻找上方的门
好让他们夏天的夹克享受微风轻送；
他们的笑声被震耳欲聋的轰鸣吞噬，
它来自被俘的风，渴望着回归田野和大海；
当地的纵帆船在沉睡的海水中漂流，
海洋冰凉又温暖，海鸥盘旋着掠过，
等待风浪将龙骨轻轻托举
在深海的岛屿之间；
岛上是开满白色花朵的高大棕榈，
把它们的芬芳借给热带海洋，
田野在露水浸润的夜晚静卧，
商船在它们的上方漂浮，新鲜又自由。

Block City

by Robert Louis Stevenson

What are you able to build with your blocks?
Castles and palaces, temples and docks.
Rain may keep raining, and others go roam,
But I can be happy and building at home.

Let the sofa be mountains, the carpet be sea,
There I'll establish a city for me:
A kirk and a mill and a palace beside,
And a harbor as well where my vessels may ride.

Great is the palace with pillar and wall,
A sort of a tower on top of it all,
And steps coming down in an orderly way
To where my toy vessels lie safe in the bay.

This one is sailing and that one is moored:
Hark to the song of the sailors on board!
And see on the steps of my palace, the kings
Coming and going with presents and things!

积木城市

[英国] 罗伯特·路易斯·史蒂文森

你能用你的积木建造什么？
城堡和宫殿，庙宇和码头。
雨也许会下个不停，别人也许会四处漫游，
但我可以在家里开开心心地建造房屋。

把沙发当作高山，把地毯当作大海，
在那里我可以为自己建座城市：
近旁有一座教堂、一座磨坊和一座宫殿，
还有一个供我的轮船停靠的海港。

用柱子和围墙盖起宏伟的宫殿，
每座的顶端都是高塔的形状，
台阶有序地蜿蜒而下
通往我的玩具轮船安歇的海湾。

这艘还在航行，那艘已经停泊：
且听船上水手的高歌！
且看在我宫殿的台阶之上，君王们
正满载着礼品，来来往往！

Sea
大海

La Mer

by Oscar Wilde

A white mist drifts across the shrouds,
A wild moon in this wintry sky
Gleams like an angry lion's eye
Out of a mane of tawny clouds.

The muffled steersman at the wheel
Is but a shadow in the gloom;
And in the throbbing engine-room
Leap the long rods of polished steel.

The shattered storm has left its trace
Upon this huge and heaving dome,
For the thin threads of yellow foam
Float on the waves like ravelled lace.

海洋

[爱尔兰] 奥斯卡 · 王尔德

白色迷雾穿越桅杆，
一轮狂月挂在冷空。
透过鬃毛般的褐色云层，
露出怒狮般的闪亮眼睛。

裹着围巾的舵手正在掌舵
不过是幽暗里的一处阴影；
在这轰隆作响的驾驶舱里，
跳动着明晃晃的长长钢条。

暴风雨在晃动的巨大穹顶上，
留下了它的一抹痕迹，
黄色泡沫的细线漂浮在海浪上，
仿佛一片散开的蕾丝。

Ocean of Forms

by Rabindranath Tagore

I dive down into the depth of the ocean of forms,
hoping to gain the perfect pearl of the formless.

No more sailing from harbor to harbor with this my weather-beaten boat.
The days are long passed when my sport was to be tossed on waves.

And now I am eager to die into the deathless.

Into the audience hall by the fathomless abyss
where swells up the music of toneless strings
I shall take this harp of my life.

I shall tune it to the notes of forever,
and when it has sobbed out its last utterance,
lay down my silent harp at the feet of the silent.

有形海洋

[印度]罗宾德拉纳特·泰戈尔

我跳进有形海洋的深处，
希望获得无形的完美珍珠。

我不再驾着我的破船从海港驶向海港。
热衷弄潮的日子早已远去。

如今我渴望死亡，进入永生的国度。

我将带上我生命的竖琴，
进入无底深渊旁的音乐大厅，
无调的音乐在那里四下回荡。

我将把曲子调成永恒，
当它呜咽着吐出最后一个音符，
我便把静谧的竖琴放在静谧的脚旁。

The Mystic Blue

by David Herbert Lawrence

Out of the darkness, fretted sometimes in its sleeping,
Jets of sparks in fountains of blue come leaping
To sight, revealing a secret, numberless secrets keeping.

Sometimes the darkness trapped within a wheel
Runs into speed like a dream, the blue of the steel
Showing the rocking darkness now a-reel.

And out of the invisible, streams of bright blue drops
Rain from the showery heavens, and bright blue crops
Surge from the under-dark to their ladder-tops.

And all the manifold blue and joyous eyes,
The rainbow arching over in the skies,

New sparks of wonder opening in surprise.

All these pure things come foam and spray of the sea
Of Darkness abundant, which shaken mysteriously,

Breaks into dazzle of living, as dolphins that leap from the sea
Of midnight shake it to fire, so the secret of death we see.

神秘的蓝色

[英国] 戴维 · 赫伯特 · 劳伦斯

来自黑暗，有时在沉睡中一阵焦躁，
蓝色喷泉中的火花喷薄而出。
目之所及，从那无数藏匿的秘密中揭晓一个谜底。

有时黑暗被困在一个轮子里，
像梦境一般骤然加速，钢铁之蓝
此刻把黑暗摇晃成一个卷轴。

从看不见的地方流出亮蓝色的水滴，
天堂洒下的雨水和亮蓝色的庄稼
从下方的黑暗涌向他们的梯顶。

所有多姿多彩的蓝色和欢乐的眼睛，
在天空架起的这弯彩虹，
新的火花在惊奇中绽放。

所有这些纯净的事物都来自大海的泡沫和浪花，

来自丰沛的黑暗，它正神秘地来回摆动。

闯入生活的斑斓，如同海豚跃出午夜的海面，

晃动着让它灼烧，我们得以窥探死亡的秘密。

As if the Sea should Part

by Emily Dickinson

As if the Sea should part
And show a further Sea—
And that—a further—and the Three
But a presumption be—

Of Periods of Seas—
Unvisited of Shores—
Themselves the Verge of Seas to be—
Eternity—is Those—

仿佛这片大海就要分开

[美国] 艾米莉 · 狄金森

仿佛这片大海就要分开
展现出一片更远的海洋——
除此之外——还有一片更远的——这三片
只是假设而已——

海洋的各个时期——
未曾造访的海岸——
它们自身就是海洋的边缘——
那些——便是永恒——

The Sea

by Dorothy Parker

Who lay against the sea, and fled,
Who lightly loved the wave,
Shall never know, when he is dead,
A cool and murmurous grave.

But in a shallow pit shall rest
For all eternity,
And bear the earth upon the breas
That once had worn the sea.

大海

[美国] 多萝西 · 帕克

谁曾背靠大海躺着，又逃之夭夭，
谁曾淡淡地爱着波涛，
再不会有人知晓这些，
待他死了，躺在低语着的冰凉坟墓里。

不过在一个浅浅的坑里
他就能永远地安息，
泥土覆盖在沥青之上，
那儿曾经被海水包裹。

By The Sea

by Christina Rossetti

Why does the sea moan evermore?
Shut out from heaven it makes its moan,
It frets against the boundary shore;
All earth's full rivers cannot fill
The sea, that drinking thirsteth still.

Sheer miracles of loveliness
Lie hid in its unlooked-on bed:
Anemones, salt, passionless,
Blow flower-like; just enough alive
To blow and multiply and thrive.

Shells quaint with curve, or spot, or spike,
Encrusted live things argus-eyed,
All fair alike, yet all unlike,
Are born without a pang, and die
Without a pang, and so pass by.

在海边

[英国] 克里斯蒂娜 · 罗塞蒂

为何大海在哀叹不止?
被天堂拒之门外让它哀叹不止，
它在岸边躁动不安;
大地上所有的河流加在一起
也不能填满大海，它仍然干渴难耐。

可爱的奇迹般的海洋生灵
躲藏在看不见的海底:
海葵、盐粒，平静安详，
像花儿一样绽开;它们的活力
只够绽放，以及繁衍生息。

带有曲线、斑点或尖刺的贝壳，
坚壳包裹的活物，目光锐利，
都很相似，又各有各的不同，
降生的时候没有剧痛，
死亡的时候亦没有剧痛，就此挥手。

The Sound of the Sea

by Henry Wadsworth Longfellow

The sea awoke at midnight from its sleep,
And round the pebbly beaches far and wide.
I heard the first wave of the rising tide
Rush onward with uninterrupted sweep;
A voice out of the silence of the deep,
A sound mysteriously multiplied.
As of a cataract from the mountain's side,
Or roar of winds upon a wooded steep.
So comes to us at times, from the unknown
And inaccessible solitudes of being,
The rushing of the sea-tides of the soul;
And inspirations, that we deem our own,
Are some divine of foreshadowing and foreseeing
Of things beyond our reason or control.

海的声音

[美国] 亨利 · 华兹华斯 · 朗费罗

午夜时分，大海从睡梦中醒来，
远远环绕着卵石密布的海滩。
我听见涨潮的第一声海浪，
一浪又一浪地向前冲刷；
从深海的寂静里传来一个声音，
那声音神秘地渐次交叠，
仿佛山涧瀑布的飞流直下，
又如密林峭壁间的狂风呼号。
存在的孤寂时常向我们袭来，
难以接近，又充满未知，
灵魂的海潮涌动不止；
还有我们自诩拥有的灵感，
不过是对超出理性与掌控之物的
某种神圣的先兆和预知。